Paddington

AT THE STATION

MICHAEL BOND
illustrated by John Lobban

HarperCollins *Publishers*

Mr. and Mrs. Brown first met Paddington on a railway platform.

In fact, that was how he came to have such an unusual name for a bear, for Paddington was the name of the station.

The Browns were there to meet their daughter, Judy, who was coming home from school for the holidays.

The station was crowded with people. Trains were whistling, taxis hooting, porters rushing about.

Mr. Brown saw him first. But there was so much noise, he had to tell his wife several times before she understood.

"A *bear*? On Paddington station? Don't be silly. There can't be!" said Mrs. Brown.

"But there *is*," said Mr. Brown. "Over there – behind those mailbags. It was wearing a funny kind of hat."

He caught hold of his wife's arm and pushed her through the crowd.

"There you are," said Mr. Brown, pointing towards a dark corner. "I told you so!"

Mrs. Brown could just see a small, furry object in the shadows. It seemed to be sitting on some kind of suitcase and around its neck there was a label with some writing on it.

"Why, Henry!" she exclaimed. "I believe you were right after all. It *is* a bear!"

She peered at it more closely. It seemed a very unusual kind of bear. It was brown in colour, a rather dirty brown, and it was wearing a duffle-coat and a most odd-looking hat, with a wide brim. From beneath the brim two large, round eyes stared back at her.

The bear stood up and politely raised its hat.

"Good afternoon," it said, in a small, clear voice.

"Er . . . good afternoon," replied Mr. Brown.

There was a moment of silence.

"Can I help you?" asked the bear.

"Well . . . no," replied Mr. Brown. "Er . . . as a matter of fact, we were wondering if we could help you."

Mrs. Brown bent down.

"You're a very small bear," she said.

The bear puffed out its chest.

"I'm a very rare sort of bear," he replied importantly. "There aren't many of us left where I come from."

"And where is that?" asked Mrs. Brown.

"Darkest Peru," whispered the bear. "I'm not really supposed to be here at all. I'm a stowaway!"

"A stowaway?" Mr. Brown looked anxiously over his shoulder. He almost expected to see a policeman standing behind him.

"Yes," said the bear. "I used to live with my Aunt Lucy in Peru, but she had to go into a home for retired bears."

"You don't mean to say you've come all the way from South America by yourself?" exclaimed Mrs. Brown.

The bear nodded.

"But whatever did you do for food?" asked Mr. Brown. "You must be starving."

Bending down, the bear unlocked the suitcase with a small key, which it also had round its neck, and brought out a jar.

"I ate marmalade," he said rather proudly. "Bears like marmalade. And I lived in a lifeboat."

"But what are you going to do now?"
asked Mr. Brown.

"Oh, I shall be all right . . . I
expect." The bear bent down to do up
its case again. As he did so Mrs.
Brown noticed the writing on the
label.

It said: PLEASE LOOK AFTER
THIS BEAR. THANK YOU.

"Oh, Henry!" she said. "What *shall* we do? We can't just leave him here. There's no knowing what might happen to him. Can't he come and stay with us for a few days?" She looked down at the bear. "He *is* rather sweet. And he'd be such company for Jonathan and Judy. They'd never forgive you if they knew you'd left him here."

Mr. Brown looked doubtful. He bent down. "Would you like to come and stay with us?" he asked. "That is, if you've nothing else planned."

The bear jumped and his hat nearly fell off with excitement. "Oooh, yes, please! I should like that very much. I've nowhere to go, really."

"Well, that's settled then," said Mrs. Brown. "And you can have marmalade for breakfast every morning."

"*Every* morning?" The bear looked as if it could hardly believe its ears. "I only had it on special occasions at home."

"Every morning starting tomorrow," said Mrs. Brown. "And honey on Sundays."

"By the way," said Mr. Brown, "you'd better know our names. This is Mrs. Brown and I'm Mr. Brown."

The bear raised its hat politely – twice. "I haven't really got a name," he said. "Not an English one."

"Then we'd better give you one," said Mrs. Brown. "It ought to be something special. I know what! We found you on Paddington station so we'll call you Paddington!"

"Paddington!" The bear repeated it several times to make sure.

Mrs. Brown stood up. "Good. Now, Paddington, I have to meet our little daughter, Judy, off the train. I'm sure you must be thirsty after your long journey, so you go along to the buffet with Mr. Brown and he'll buy you a nice cup of tea."

Paddington licked his lips. "I'm *very* thirsty," he said. He picked up his suitcase and pulled his hat down firmly over his head.

"Now, Henry, look after him," Mrs. Brown called after them. "And for goodness' sake, take that label off his neck. It makes him look like a parcel."

Mr. Brown found a table for two in a corner of the buffet.

By standing on a chair, Paddington could just rest his paws comfortably on the top.

"Well, Paddington," said Mr. Brown, as he placed two steaming cups of tea on the table and a plate piled high with cakes, "how's that to be going on with?"

Paddington's eyes glistened. "It's very nice, thank you. Do you think anyone would mind if I stood on the table to eat?"

Before Mr. Brown could answer he had climbed up and placed his right paw firmly on a bun. It was a very large bun, the biggest and stickiest of all, and in a matter of moments most of the inside found its way on to Paddington's whiskers.

Mr. Brown stirred his tea and looked out of the window, pretending he had tea with a bear on Paddington station every day of his life.

"Henry!" It was Mrs. Brown's voice. "Henry, whatever are you doing to that poor bear? Look at him! He's covered all over with cream and jam and he's got his nose stuck in a paper cup!"

Mr. Brown jumped up in confusion. "He seemed rather hungry," he answered.

Mrs. Brown turned to her daughter. "This is what happens when I leave your father alone for five minutes."

Judy clapped her hands excitedly. "Oh, Daddy, is he really going to stay with us?"

Paddington suddenly became aware that people were talking about him. He looked up to see that Mrs. Brown had been joined by a small girl. He jumped up, meaning to raise his hat, and in his haste slipped on a patch of strawberry jam. He waved his paws wildly in the air and then, before anyone could catch him, he somersaulted backwards and landed with a splash with one foot in his cup of tea. The tea was still very hot and he jumped up again and promptly stepped into Mr. Brown's cup.

Judy laughed until the tears rolled down her face. "Oh, Mummy, isn't he funny!" she cried. "He looks as though he's wearing wellington boots!"

"You wouldn't think," said Mrs. Brown, "that anyone could get in such a mess in so short a time."

Paddington took off his hat and started to fill it with the remains of the cakes.

Mr. Brown coughed. "Perhaps," he said, "we'd better go. I'll see if I can find a taxi."

Paddington stepped gingerly off the table and Judy took one of his paws. "Come along," she said. "We'll take you home and you can have a nice hot bath. Then you can tell me all about South America."

When they came out of the buffet Mr. Brown had already found a taxi and he waved them across.

The driver looked hard at Paddington and then at the inside of his nice clean taxi.

"Bears is sixpence extra," he said, gruffly. "Sticky bears is ninepence!"

"He can't help being sticky, driver," said Mr. Brown. "He's just had a nasty accident."

The driver hesitated. "All right, 'op in."

Paddington stood on a tip-up seat behind the driver so that he could see out of the window. Mr. Brown leaned forward. "Number thirty-two, Windsor Gardens."

The driver cupped his ear with one hand. "Can't 'ear you," he shouted.

Paddington tapped him on the shoulder. "Number thirty-two, Windsor Gardens," he repeated.

The taxi driver jumped at the sound of Paddington's voice and narrowly missed hitting a bus.

He looked down at his shoulder and glared. "Cream!" he said. "All over me new coat!"

"Oh, dear," thought Paddington, "I'm in trouble again."

Judy giggled and gave his paw a friendly squeeze.

"I think I'm going to like staying with the Browns," thought Paddington.

Carnival is an imprint of
HarperCollins Publishers Ltd
77-85 Fulham Palace Road,
Hammersmith, London W6 8JB

First published by Carnival 1988
This edition first published 1992

Text © 1976 Michael Bond
Illustrations © 1992 HarperCollinsPublishers Ltd

ISBN 0 00 192623 3

Printed in Great Britain by
BPCC Hazell Books, Paulton and Aylesbury